Ditherus Wart
Accidental Gladiator

Alan MacDonald

illustrations by Mark Beech

BLOOMSBURY

Captain
Custardly Wart

Ditherus
Wart

Sir Bigwart

Wart

Tyler
Wart

Lord 'Bingo'
Bottomley Wart

Honesty
Wart

Sharper
Wart

The Wart family tree.....

First published in Great Britain in 2008 by Bloomsbury Publishing Plc
36 Soho Square, London, W1D 3QY

A CIP catalogue record of this book is available from the British Library

ISBN 978 0 7475 9466 6

All papers used by Bloomsbury Publishing are natural, recyclable products made
from wood grown in well-managed forests. The manufacturing processes conform to
the environmental regulations of the country of origin.

Printed in Great Britain by Clays Ltd, St Ives Plc

1 3 5 7 9 10 8 6 4 2

www.bloomsbury.com

It's Behind You!

Foreword

by

Professor Frank Lee Barking (M. A. D. Phil)

S ince the dawn of time members of the hapless Wart family have been dogged by disaster. From facing flesh-eating ogres to grappling with gladi-ators and being kidnapped by pirates, Warts have looked Death in the eye and lived to tell the tale. Now, thanks to years of painstaking research, and literally hours of daydreaming, I am proud to bring you the absolutely true and epic saga of ...

The History of Warts

Chapter 1
A Nasty Plot

Porcus Maximus IV, noble Caesar, Emperor of Rome, sat back in his golden throne. It was a tight fit. Lately his throne had got smaller or else his rear had got bigger, which for someone with the mightiest bottom in Rome was a growing problem.

'Sorry, Marcus,' he yawned. 'What were you saying?'

'I was speaking of the war, Your Excellency,' said Marcus Furius. As Captain of the Imperial Guard,

Furius protected the Emperor and advised him on matters he didn't understand. In Porcus Maximus's case, this covered pretty much everything.

'Ah, the war, good, and how is it coming along?' asked Porcus.

'Very badly,' said Marcus Furius.

'Oh dear! Badly? Remind me, who are we fighting at the moment?'

'The Gauls.'

'And they live in?'

'Gaul, Your Mightiness.'

'Ah yes, of course,' said Porcus, who hadn't the faintest clue where Gaul was. Like his bottom, the Roman Empire was expanding all the time and he found it difficult to keep up. 'But surely,' he said, 'we're meant to win the war or what is the point of us invading in the first place?'

'As always Your Majesty is right,' said Furius.

'Yes, of course I'm right, but why are we losing? It's very upsetting, Furius. Surely a bunch of girls can't be that hard to beat.'

'Gauls not girls, Majesty,' sighed Furius. 'There is a slight difference.'

'Yes, yes,' said Porcus. 'But I am the Emperor and

if we start losing wars it makes me look an idiot.'

Furius was tempted to say the Emperor didn't need any help looking an idiot but instead he rubbed his chin, and pretended to think.

'Perhaps, Your Worthiness, it could be the fault of your general,' he suggested with a sly, sideways look.

'Ah, the general. He's like the team captain, isn't he? The one who decides which end we're shooting into.'

'Something like that, Majesty.' Furius nodded.

'And who is our team captain at the moment?' asked Porcus.

Marcus Furius narrowed his eyes. 'I believe Caius Wart is leading our army.'

'Wart?' said the Emperor. 'And what nincompoop put him in charge?'

'You did, oh Gracious One. If you recall, I humbly offered my services but you felt Wart was a better choice.'

'Did I? Ah. Hmm.' Porcus blew out his cheeks. 'Well, I've no doubt I was right, I usually am, after all I'm the Emperor and that makes me practically a god!' He attempted to rise but found his god-like bottom was stuck fast.

'Of course a truly *great* ruler sometimes changes his mind,' suggested Furius.

'What?' said Porcus, still struggling to escape from his throne.

'I was thinking, Your Honour, it's not too late to remove Wart and promote someone else. Someone older, wiser, better-looking,' said Furius, turning sideways to offer his best profile.

'No, no one springs to mind,' replied Porcus. 'And

besides, I'm sure Caius will beat these girls in the end, even if they are quite tough. He's a splendid fellow, Caius, brave, clever, loyal – you could learn a lot from him, Furius.'

'Yes, Your Flabbiness,' muttered Furius.

'Pardon?'

'I said yes, Your Fabulousness.'

'Now do help me up, it's time for my morning bath,' said the Emperor. 'I've ordered extra bubbles today.'

Furius reached out a hand to his master and tried to prise him from his throne. It took a great deal of heaving and grunting before he finally shot out and landed on top of the Captain, flattening him like a folding deckchair.

'Have that throne seen to,' puffed the Emperor, 'it needs letting out a bit. And by the way, where am I eating tonight?' (Most nights Porcus Maximus dined out as a guest of one of his subjects. He liked to be seen in public and, besides, it saved him money.)

'I believe Hilaria Wart has invited you to supper,' replied Furius.

'Oh, Hilaria. Do I know her?'

'The wife of Caius Wart.'

'Excellent! And will he be there too?'

'No, Majesty, he is in Gaul with the army.'

'Pity!' said Porcus. 'Splendid fellow, Caius, and his sons – all splendid too. Titus, Smitus and . . . um what's the youngest one called?'

'Ditherus, Majesty,' said Marcus Furius.

'Yes, that's the one. Now back to important matters, Marcus: what in the name of Jupiter shall I wear tonight? Perhaps I should go in disguise? Remember the fun we had with Vesuvius when I arrived at his house dressed as Hades![1]'

Marcus Furius waited until the Emperor had left the room, and snapped his fingers. Instantly a sinister-looking man dressed in black stepped out of the shadows, where he had been lurking for some time. Furius whispered in his ear and the man's wrinkled face broke into a cruel smile. A moment later he left, hiding something under his dark robe.

Furius watched him go. If his plan succeeded,

---

1 Hades – Roman god of the underworld. Hades was also the name given to the kingdom of the dead. (In other words it was Hell.)

Wart would no longer stand in his way. Then the path would be clear for him, Marcus Furius, to become the most powerful man in Rome – apart from the Emperor of course, who had the brain of a turnip.

Chapter 2

Down a Dark Alley

Ditherus Wart didn't know he was about to be drawn into a dark and dangerous plot. In fact he was just thinking how nothing really exciting ever happened to him. Two months ago his father and brothers had ridden off to fight the war in Gaul. Ditherus had begged to go along but as usual his dad said he was too young. Someone had to stay behind to look after his mother and the tortoise. So Ditherus remained at home, dreaming of the day he would be old enough to do something brave and heroic.

To make matters even worse, it turned out that the Emperor was coming to supper.

'Not the Emperor!' moaned Ditherus, when his mother told him.

'Yes, darling, we're very lucky he wishes to honour us.'

'I don't see what's so lucky about it.' Ditherus scowled. 'Last time he stayed for hours and then he was sick in the fountain.'

'Dumpling, do try to understand,' sighed Hilaria, 'the Emperor is terribly important and if he's sick in our fountain that is also a great honour.'

Ditherus said nothing. It wasn't the throwing up he minded – most Romans burped, puked and farted their way through meals[2] – what he hated was having to endure a whole evening of Porcus Maximus talking about his favourite subject: Porcus Maximus.

---

2 Romans believed being sick was Nature's way of making room for seconds. Rich houses had a **Vomitorium** set aside for the purpose.

Worse still, Marcus Furius would be there, and he was as grim as a gargoyle and twice as ugly.

Ditherus realised his mother's lips were moving which meant she was still talking.

'. . . and that's why I need you to take Tidio to the market and buy a few things for supper.'

'Me?' said Ditherus. 'Why do I have to go?'

'Because, pumpkin, the Emperor is coming and I have a million and one things to do. I haven't even decided which earrings I'm going to wear.'

Hilaria held out a wax tablet with her shopping list. 'Now stay with Tidio and don't talk to any strangers. And please, please, darling, try to keep out of trouble!'

Ditherus couldn't see how anyone could get into trouble at a market.

The square was bustling with people when they arrived. Ditherus breathed in the rich smells of sausages, smoke, spices and the salty whiff of fish laced with the general stink of sweaty bodies. He pushed his way through the crowd with his loyal slave, Tidio, beside him.

Tidio spotted a stall selling stuffed dormice and

was soon haggling over the price. Tired of waiting, Ditherus seized the chance to slip away down a
side street where the stalls looked more interesting.
Tunics and togas fluttered in the wind like flags, and
soothsayers tugged at his sleeve, offering to tell his
fortune. Porcus Maximus's vacant face beamed back
at him on everything from tapestries to Roman bath
mats.

11

Ditherus felt a hand land lightly on his shoulder and spun round. A stooped old man, dressed from head to foot in black robes, bowed to him. His hood hid everything but his wrinkled monkey face and he smiled, revealing yellow teeth.

'You look for somethings?' he asked, wrapping a friendly arm round Ditherus's shoulder.

'Me? No.'

'Yes,' nodded monkey man, 'I have for you! Very good!'

From under his robe he produced something wrapped in a rich crimson cloth. He drew a fold back for a second and a flash of silver caught the light.

'What is it?' asked Ditherus, intrigued.

'Come, come! I show you,' said the man, beckoning with a crooked finger.

'Oh, I can't. I'm meant to stay with my slave.'

'Him slave? Him boss you about?'

'No,' said Ditherus. 'Him not boss me about. I do what I like.'

'Good, you come,' insisted the old man. He led the way between the stalls, glancing back all the time, smiling and nodding.

'Where are we going?' called Ditherus as he tried

to keep up. He looked around. The stranger had vanished. A hand suddenly beckoned from the dark shadows of an alley.

'Here! You come! Come!'

Ditherus hesitated. Stepping into a dark alley after a stranger was probably not a good idea. He might be a thief or a murderer or worse (though he couldn't think exactly what would be worse). But Ditherus had glimpsed something in that red cloth and curiosity got the better of him. He turned into the alley where the peddler was already unwrapping the cloth.

'See! For you!' He grinned crazily.

Ditherus took it in his hands. It was a *gladius*, a short sword – spotted with age and possibly blood. The hilt had a silver serpent curled round the letter B.

'This sword very good,' nodded monkey man. 'Is *grannyator*.'

'Grannyator?' said Ditherus.

'Yes, big famous. Fight other grannyator.'

'Oh, it's a *gladiator*'s sword?'

'Yes, yes. Gradeeeator. Very good!' Monkey man danced around pretending he was a gladiator fighting off a whole army. It seemed to make him out of breath. He leaned on a wall and pointed at Ditherus. 'Now you.'

Ditherus raised the sword. It felt good – light, balanced. Even grasping it in his hand he felt taller, stronger, more heroic than usual. He tried a few tentative swishes in the air.

Monkey man clapped and grinned. 'Yes, yes! You make good gradeeeator! She is for you.'

'You think so?' Ditherus tried a lunge at his own shadow.

Footsteps approached down the alley. Ditherus spun round, forgetting the sword in his hand, and Tidio leapt backwards in surprise.

'Careful, master! That thing is sharp!'

'Sorry, Tidio. It's a sword.'

'I can see that. Where did you get it?'

'I met this, er . . . fellow. I think he wants to sell it.'

The old peddler nodded his head eagerly. 'This sword good. I give you very good price.'

'Please, master, we're late,' said Tidio. 'I don't think you need a sword.'

'My brothers both have swords,' argued Ditherus.

'That's different; they're soldiers! Anyway you don't know how to use one.'

'I do! I've been learning!'

Ditherus had spent hours poring over *The Big Book of Gladiators*, which had a double-page spread on swordplay for beginners with helpful diagrams.

'Master, what if your mother sees it?'

'She won't!'

The peddler was getting impatient. 'Twenty denarii[3],' he said.

'Ridiculous!' scoffed Tidio.

---

3 **Denarii** – A denarius was a silver coin, worth a day's wages.

'Sixteen,' countered the peddler, who had no objection to haggling.

'Please, Tidio. It belonged to a gladiator.'

Tidio examined the blade. 'It's certainly ancient – this looks like rust.'

'Very nice sword. Fourteen denarii,' said monkey man, leaning in close.

'Ugh! His breath is worse than a camel's!' said Tidio.

'Yes, very nice,' winked the peddler. 'Twelve.'

'We don't want it.'

'Ten.'

Ditherus had pulled out his purse and was checking the contents. 'I've only got five.'

'Five is good.' Monkey man snatched the coins and they disappeared into the folds of his black robe. He bowed to them with his palms pressed together, then turned and darted along the alleyway. Seconds later he had vanished, though whether he'd slipped through a door or scuttled down a hole neither of them knew.

'Well! He was in a great hurry,' remarked Tidio.

Ditherus was too busy examining his new sword to listen. He moved out of the alley to get a better look at it. There was something written on the blade, though the letters were difficult to make out.

'Master, do me one favour,' said Tidio, leaping aside.

'What?'

'Next time you're going to practise, tell me, then I can wear a helmet.'

Chapter 3

Hail Caesar!

By the time they reached home Hilaria was pacing the room in a state of panic.

'Where in Hades have you been?' she demanded. 'I've had to plump the cushions all by myself!'

'I beg your pardon, mistress,' said Tidio.

'It was my fault,' added Ditherus.

'Well, don't just stand there like a pair of nodding donkeys. Tidio, take the food to the kitchen. Ditherus, what's in that bag?'

'This?' Ditherus looked flustered. 'Um nothing ... just fruit.'

'Yes, fruit – figs, apples, dates – fruity fruit,' gabbled Tidio.

'Then put it on a plate!' said Hilaria impatiently.

Ditherus began to pile fruit on to a plate. He could see the sword nestled at the bottom of his bag.

But before he could smuggle it into his room, he was interrupted by a loud banging on the door.

Hilaria gasped. 'The Emperor! Darling, how do I look?'

Ditherus blinked. His mother was wearing so much gold and jewellery he was surprised she didn't collapse under the weight. 'You look, er ... shiny,' he said.

Tidio opened the door and Marcus Furius marched in, followed by four of his soldiers. He bowed stiffly.

'Good evening,' he glowered. 'The emperor sends his apologies. He asked me to tell you he may be a little late.' Ditherus noticed he said this like a bad actor reciting his lines while his eyes flicked to the big soldier by the door, who was smirking like an overgrown schoolboy. The soldier's helmet was way too small for him and his belly bulged under his breastplate. There was something about his round, piggy face that was oddly familiar.

An awkward silence fell. Marcus Furius often had this effect on entering a room.

'So, Marcus, how are you?' asked Hilaria, to break the silence.

'Well enough,' growled the Captain.

Another silence.

Furius looked around him. 'You won't object if my men search the house?'

'Search? Whatever for?' asked Hilaria.

'One can't be too careful. You never know where *enemies* may be lurking.' His eye for some reason fell on Ditherus, whose cheeks flushed even though he hadn't done anything.

'Please. Look all you like,' shrugged Hilaria.

Furius nodded to his guards, who began poking in cupboards and lifting up rugs. Ditherus's eyes darted to his bag on the floor.

The plump guard was waddling around making a show of picking up cushions and looking absurdly pleased with himself. Ditherus thought it was odd that Marcus Furius hadn't noticed that one of his soldiers had a bottom the size of a house.

Hilaria, meanwhile, was trying to keep the conversation going.

'Well, hasn't it been hot?' she remarked. 'Do you find it hot, Marcus?'

'It makes no difference to me,' snapped Furius.

'But surely, wearing all that heavy armour. Doesn't it get, well, a little sweaty?'

'Nothing wrong with sweat,' replied Furius. 'Sweat is the mark of a soldier. You should smell the sweat of an army going into battle.'

'Goodness!' said Hilaria, who felt she would probably rather not.

There was another long silence. Ditherus was edging closer to his bag. If he bent down slowly, he could pick it up without attracting attention.

'And the Emperor, I hope he is well?' asked Hilaria, changing the subject.

'Oh, never better!' said the plump soldier unexpectedly, then burst into giggles when everyone looked at him.

Ditherus now had the bag in his hand. All he had to do was figure a way to sneak out of the room. The plump soldier was helping himself to grapes and had red juice dribbling down his chins. Ditherus suddenly remembered where he'd seen that moonish face before. Last time the owner was being sick in the fountain. Porcus Maximus (for it was he) caught him staring and turned pink, starting to splutter and cough. A grape had slipped down the wrong way. In a moment Marcus Furius was at his side, banging him on the back.

'Your Worthiness! Are you all right? Shall I fetch some water?'

Porcus Maximus held up a hand while he got his breath back. 'Hilaria, my dear, I fear I am discovered. It is I, your noble Emperor!' He took off his helmet and beamed at them all. Hilaria raised her hands in astonishment.

'Your Majesty! What a surprise!'

'Ha ha!' chortled Porcus. 'What do you think of my little disguise? I borrowed the costume from Marcus here. Ha ha ha!'

Everyone (apart from Ditherus) thought the

Emperor's disguise was amazing. They had never seen anyone look quite as soldierly and handsome. Porcus settled himself on a couch and started to work his way through the food on the table, talking all the while. Ditherus saw his chance to slip away at last, but luck was against him. Just as he reached the door, his mother looked up.

'Ditherus, dumpling, come and join us!'

'Oh, there you are, young Didderus!' beamed Porcus Maximus, who up to now had assumed the boy was one of the servants.

Ditherus hesitated. If he tried to leave now, it would look like an insult to the Emperor. There was nothing for it but to go back.

'Come here, boy. I'm not going to eat you!' Porcus beckoned a plump finger.

Ditherus wasn't so sure, but approached and bowed low. He shifted the bag behind his back.

'Majesty, you remember my son?' said Hilaria proudly.

'Of course,' said Porcus, who remembered Titus and Smitus much better and was wondering if this son had shrunk in the wash. He held out a dimpled hand and Ditherus bent to kiss it.

'WAIT!' interrupted Marcus Furius. 'What's in the bag?'

The colour drained from Ditherus's face. 'Nothing.'

'Good. Then you won't mind showing me.'

Furius fished inside the bag and brought out the crimson cloth. The sword slipped out and fell on the marble floor with a loud clang. There was a shocked silence.

'I can explain . . .' began Ditherus.

'Really?' Marcus Furius was smiling coldly as he handed the sword to the Emperor.

'By the beard of Jupiter!' exclaimed Porcus. 'I know this sword!'

Furius nodded. 'A Nemesis II, Excellency. Only one man owned a sword like this – Brutalus the Bold.'

'Brutalus?' said Hilaria.

'The greatest gladiator in Roman history,' said Marcus Furius. 'Thirty-seven fights, thirty-seven wins – which is why every collector in Rome would like to own this sword. See the words on the blade? *Mors Et Wimpum* – Death is for Sissies. If you believe the legend, whoever fights with this sword is invincible.' His eyes glittered as he held it to the light.

'But I still don't understand. What is my Ditherus doing with it?' asked Hilaria.

'A good question,' replied Furius. 'Particularly since it was stolen from the Emperor himself.'

'Stolen?' croaked Ditherus.

'Most upsetting,' said the Emperor. 'It was taken from my collection last week.'

Ditherus felt his legs turn to jelly. This was definitely not good. Not good at all. Stealing was a crime, but stealing from the Emperor himself . . . only someone desperate or stupid would do that, which explained why everyone in the room was staring at him as if he was desperate or stupid.

'Ditherus, you big silly!' said Hilaria. 'What are you doing with the Emperor's sword?'

'Yes. Do explain.' Furius looked as if he was enjoying this.

'I got it from the market . . . the man . . . the man at the market,' stammered Ditherus.

'Which man?'

'I don't know! I've never met him before.'

'What was his name?'

'I . . . I don't remember.'

Furius snorted. 'He's lying, Your Majesty. The boy is a common thief.'

'Oh, pumpkin, really!' tutted Hilaria.

'But, Mum, I didn't . . . I bought it for five denarii.'

'FIVE DENARII!' exploded Furius. 'For this – a priceless sword from the Emperor's personal collection?'

'It's true!'

'Lies!' spat Furius. 'You stole the sword and hid it in your bag. And I'll tell you why – because you were planning to *murder the Emperor*!'

Ditherus's mouth fell open. Everyone looked shocked. Not least the Emperor, who was so astonished he even stopped eating for a moment.

'Marcus,' he blinked. 'You surely don't think . . . ?'

'Your Innocence, the sword was in his bag,' said Furius. 'What further proof do you need? Guards – ARREST THIS BOY!'

Two brawny soldiers seized Ditherus by the arm, lifting him off the ground.

'No wait!' pleaded Ditherus. 'Mum, tell them!'

Hilaria turned to the Emperor. 'Really, Your Highness. Couldn't you just send him to bed without any supper?'

'Yes, Marcus, couldn't I?' asked Porcus, reaching for a chicken leg.

Furius shook his head firmly. 'The law is perfectly clear, Excellency.'

'Is it?' asked the Emperor, who usually found the law very complicated.

'Treason is a serious offence. The punishment is death. Take him away!'

Ditherus was dragged kicking and struggling into the hall.

'Tidio. Tell them!' he cried. 'You were there! Tell them what happened!'

Tidio hurried after them and laid a hand on Marcus Furius's arm. 'Please,' he begged. 'You're making a terrible mistake.'

Furius shook off his hand violently. 'And who are you?'

'Me? I'm just a slave,' said Tidio.

'Then you should know better than to touch an officer of His Majesty's guard,' stormed Furius. 'Arrest this man!'

One of the soldiers grabbed hold of Tidio by the scruff of the neck and dragged him along as the procession swept out of the door.

Hilaria stood at the gate, waving her hanky, as they marched off down the road.

'Don't worry, pumpkin!' she called. 'Trust in the gods. I'm sure it will all turn out fine!'

Chapter 4

Things Look Grim

The iron door swung shut with an echoing clang and the key turned in the lock. The jailer, a man who smelled as if he'd never heard of Roman baths, gave them a toothless grin and limped off up the stone steps, humming tunelessly to himself. Ditherus waited for his eyes to adjust to the darkness. The stone floor was strewn with straw, mud and something that looked like rats' droppings. In the far corner under a tiny, barred window was a heap of filthy sacks. Otherwise the dingy cell was empty.

'Well,' said Ditherus brightly. 'Things could be worse.'

Tidio shot him a look.

'I'm sure we won't be here long,' Ditherus went on. 'As soon as the Emperor sees his mistake, he'll have us released. He's not *that* stupid?'

Tidio made no answer. Actually, Porcus Maximus was amazingly stupid. He needed the advice of six ministers just to get dressed in the morning.

Tidio paced up and down rather stiffly, trying to think.

'Master,' he said. 'The man at the market, had you seen him before?'

'No,' said Ditherus. 'Why?'

'Well, doesn't it strike you as odd? You bump into a complete stranger who just *happens* to be selling a priceless sword.'

'It was a stroke of luck,' admitted Ditherus.

'And then it turns out this sword was stolen from the Emperor himself.'

'I know,' said Ditherus. 'What are the chances of that?'

'Exactly.' Tidio nodded. 'So what if it wasn't bad luck? What if someone *meant* you to buy the sword?'

Ditherus thought it over. It sort of made sense. But there wasn't time to discuss it because at that moment the jailer reappeared.

'Supper,' said Odium, pushing a plate of black bread and a jug of water under the door. Ditherus grabbed the plate hungrily. But before he could eat anything, the heap of sacks in the corner rose up, revealing that it wasn't a heap of sacks, but a red-bearded giant dressed in filthy rags. The giant grabbed the plate off him.

'MEAT!' he roared.

'Well, not exactly, but you're welcome to share . . .' began Ditherus. The bread disappeared into the giant's mouth in one gulp and he washed it down with the entire jug of water, much of it running down into his thick, tangled beard.

'That's Bladderax,' the jailer grinned. 'I wouldn't argue with him. Nasty tempers, these barbarians.'

Bladderax finished the water, tossed the jug aside and belched like a thunderclap.

'Meat! MEAT!' he thundered.

Odium shook his head. 'Now, now, Bladdy, you know there's only bread.'

'WANT MEAT!' roared the giant. 'I HUNGRY!' He threw the plate at the door and it bounced off with an ear-splitting clang. The noise startled a rat and sent it scurrying across the floor. Bladderax pounced on it in an instant. There was a crunch as he bit off the head and began chewing it noisily.

'Eugh!' said Ditherus, turning away.

'What about our supper?' asked Tidio.

'He ate it.' Odium grinned. 'Got an appetite, that one.' He collected the empty jug and turned to go.

'Wait!' Ditherus begged. 'What's going to happen to us?'

'Ah, well, that depends.' Odium stroked a spot on his chin. 'If you're lucky, they'll forget all about you. You could be in prison for years and years, like Bladdy there.'

Ditherus glanced over at the barbarian, who was picking bones out of his teeth. His beard was so long it hung over his belly.

'And if we're not lucky?' asked Ditherus.

'Then they put you to death. Still, cheer up, it might never happen. My mother always said smile and the world smiles with you.' Odium grinned at them toothlessly.

'But what about our trial?' persisted Ditherus.

'Trial?' The jailer looked blank.

'You know – where we get a chance to prove we're innocent.'

The jailer shook his head. 'Never heard of it. Who wants to listen to criminals complaining? Anyway the Tribune decides if you're innocent.'

'Then let me see the Tribune. Who is he?'

'Marcus Furius,' replied Odium.

Ditherus groaned.

The jailer had started back up the stairs, then paused and turned back.

'Oh, almost forgot, there was a lady asking to see you. Rich. Nice teeth. What was the name? Hysteria ...'

'Hilaria!' cried Ditherus. 'Tidio, we're saved! She's come to get us out!'

As usual, Ditherus's mother took a long time coming to the point. She'd brought some cheese and olives on sticks left over from supper. Tidio and Ditherus ate hungrily as they talked.

'The Emperor's really very upset,' she sighed.

'*He's* upset?' said Ditherus. 'Mum, I'm in prison!'

'I know, dear, I don't know *what* the neighbours will think. Try not to cram so many olives into your mouth at once.'

Ditherus tried to stay calm. 'Did you speak to the Emperor?' he asked.

'Well, of course I spoke to him, pumpkin. He was

at our house. It would be rude not to speak to him.'

'But about the sword. Tidio thinks we were tricked.'

'Well, if you will go buying second-hand swords, I'm not surprised,' said Hilaria.

'Mum, you have to convince the Emperor I'm innocent.'

'I told you he's upset, dear. It turns out he's been collecting gladiators' swords ever since he was seven, although personally I can't see why you would.'

'But is he going to release us?'

'Well, not at the moment. He's still terribly cross that you stole his sword.'

'I didn't STEAL IT!' cried Ditherus.

'There's no need to shout at me,' said Hilaria huffily. 'I'm just trying to help. Now, listen, I've written to your dad; he'll know what to do.'

'Dad? But he's in Gaul!' said Ditherus.

'Well, I know that, silly. I was there when we waved him off.'

'Mum! It could take *weeks* for a letter to reach him.'

'Sometimes we have to be patient,' advised Hilaria. 'And meanwhile, we trust in the gods.' She got up to go. 'I shall pray for you at the temple tomorrow. Make sure you're eating enough and remember to wash behind your ears. Tidio, I'm relying on you to see he does. Goodbye, pumpkin, I'll pop in tomorrow. And try not to look so *worried*.' Hilaria gave his hand a last squeeze, blew a kiss and was gone.

Ditherus dragged himself across the cell and lay down on the hard stone block. Bladderax was snoring steadily in the corner.

'We're never going to get out, are we?' he sighed.

Tidio began pacing again. He hadn't sat down since they'd arrived.

'Tidio, what is that lump?' asked Ditherus.

'Which lump?'

'That lump on your back.'

'Oh, you mean this?'

Tidio did something uncomfortable which involved fishing around under his tunic and a great deal of wriggling. When he straightened up he was holding a sword.

Ditherus stared in astonishment. 'You've had that all the time?'

'Yes, master. I picked it up when the soldiers were

dragging you off. I had a feeling it might come in handy.'

'But why didn't you say so before?'

'I was waiting for the right moment.' Tidio rubbed his bottom gingerly. 'You have no idea how sharp that sword is. I won't be able to sit down for a week.'

'Tidio, don't you see what this means? We're saved! We can escape!'

Tidio nodded. 'I'm relieved to hear it, master. This

cell is really quite damp. So tell me, what is your plan?'

'Plan? Oh, my plan. Right.' Ditherus had rather hoped Tidio was the one with a plan. 'Well,' he said, 'we'll use the sword, obviously. Maybe we could tunnel our way out.'

'That might take some time, master,' said Tidio. 'Perhaps your plan involves our friend the jailer?'

'Does it?' said Ditherus.

'Yes, and the bunch of keys he keeps on his belt.'

'The keys, of course!' said Ditherus. 'All we have to do is wait for the jailer to come back, force him to hand over the keys and make our escape.'

'An excellent plan, master,' said Tidio. 'I wish I had thought of it myself.'

'Thanks,' said Ditherus, who found he was much better at thinking of plans when Tidio was around.

There was only one small problem. While he'd read a lot of books about swords, Ditherus had never actually used one. Mostly he'd practised with sticks, cutting the heads off nettles and dandelions. Still, he told himself it couldn't be that difficult. All he had to do was prod the jailer in the stomach with the pointy bit and demand the keys. If he was ever going to be a hero, it was time to get in some practice. It was either that or starve to death in prison with a rat-eating barbarian for company. He gripped the Nemesis, swishing it through the air a few times. Once more he felt an odd tingling sensation, as if the sword had a strange effect on him. Then again it might have been that he needed the toilet.

'Right,' he said, trying to sound confident. 'This is how we'll do it. Next time the jailer comes in, you keep him talking, Tidio. I will hide behind the door and take him by surprise.'

'And if there are guards upstairs?' asked Tidio.

'Then we'll just have to fight our way out.'

'Yes, master, I was afraid you'd say that.'

They settled down to wait for the jailer to return. Hours passed. Through the barred window, Ditherus could see the sky growing dark and the stars coming out. He suddenly felt overcome by weariness. It had been a long day – the most exciting day of his life, though maybe exciting wasn't quite the right word. Bladderax was still asleep in the far corner. Tidio was hunched against the wall, his eyelids drooping. Ditherus lay down on the stone floor to rest. He wouldn't sleep because he needed to stay alert, ready to strike the moment the jailer returned. He would only close his eyes for a minute or two . . .

Chapter 5

Something's Burning

'Uhhh? What's happening?'

Someone had gripped Ditherus roughly by the arm and was lifting him into the air. His eyes blinked open. He had a close-up of the dusty floor as he was dragged across it by two beefy prison guards. This did not strike him as promising. A moment ago he had been fast asleep, dreaming he was riding a white horse into battle at the head of the Ninth Legion, now he was heading down a dark corridor at breakneck speed. He caught sight of a pair of pale, thin legs ahead of him. The guards had Tidio too. Behind him he could hear cries and curses and roars of fury. Someone had evidently made the mistake of waking Bladderax.

Outside, Ditherus's eyes blinked in the bright morning sunlight. They were in a narrow yard, surrounded by a high wall. Although it was baking hot someone had been to the trouble of building a couple of bonfires. *Excellent*, thought Ditherus, *perhaps we're having sausages for breakfast*.

'Ah, good morning,' said Odium pleasantly. 'Sorry to drag you out of bed but we're in a bit of a rush.'

'What's going on?' asked Ditherus.

'We're executing you,' the jailer said, smiling.

'WHAT?' said Ditherus.

'I know it's a bit sudden, but orders is orders. Marcus Furius doesn't want you cluttering up the cells. I was for giving you a proper execution, something for the family to remember, but he didn't want any fuss. "Burn them," he said.'

Ditherus stared at the two wooden poles surrounded by a pile of wood and twigs. 'You . . . you can't do this!' he stammered.

'Really, if it was up to me, I wouldn't,' sighed the jailer. 'Burnings are terrible. My clothes will stink of smoke for days on end!'

Five minutes later Ditherus and Tidio were bound to one of the poles, back to back.

Bladderax had a bonfire all to himself. It had taken four of the soldiers to bind him with ropes, and several of them were nursing bruises and

swollen eyes. Odium approached with a burning torch in his hand.

'Master!' Tidio whispered. 'Now would be a good time.'

'What are you talking about?'

'The sword. Cut the ropes!'

Ditherus let out a long groan.

'Tell me you didn't,' begged Tidio.

'I left it in the cell.'

Tidio let his head droop forward. 'Why didn't you keep it with you?'

'I fell asleep!' said Ditherus. 'I wasn't expecting to be executed this morning!'

Odium squatted down, holding the torch to the twigs at the bottom of the pile. A thin wisp of smoke curled into the air. 'Damp,' he grunted. 'I told them this wood was damp.'

'We can come back another day,' offered Tidio. 'We're not in any hurry.'

'No, don't you worry. Once this dries out it'll be fine,' said Odium.

To his left Ditherus could hear Bladderax heaving and grunting, attempting to wrench his pole clean out of the ground with a superhuman effort. The twigs below their feet began to crackle and snap.

'Got any other ideas?' asked Ditherus.

'Nothing springs to mind,' replied Tidio.

The soldiers had left the yard, leaving the jailer to watch by himself. The smoke continued to rise lazily from the fire.

'It's only smouldering,' said Ditherus. 'Maybe we can blow it out?'

'I'm not sure that's a good idea,' replied Tidio.

'We've got to do something! Come on!'

They both took a deep breath and blew with all their strength. The flames flickered into life. Twigs snapped as the fire licked at them hungrily.

'Thanks, lads, that's done the trick.' Odium nodded, rubbing his hands. 'You wait, we'll have a proper blaze soon.'

Ditherus screwed up his eyes. The smoke was making them water – which was why he didn't see the stranger enter the yard.

'Gutsius, you old dog!' laughed Odium, shaking him by the hand. 'What brings you here?'

'Business,' replied the newcomer. His head was smooth as a brown egg and his deep, booming voice bounced off the walls.

'Master!' hissed Tidio. 'Who's that?'

'I can't see!' moaned Ditherus, through clouds of smoke.

'Listen! They're talking!'

Ditherus strained to catch the conversation. The two men seemed to be bargaining over something. The one called Gutsius was waving his hands and shouting as if he thought the jailer was stone deaf.

'STRONG ONES, mind you. Not the MILK-SOPS you sold me last time.'

'He's buying slaves,' said Tidio excitedly. 'Master, the gods have heard our prayers. They're going to spare us!'

'They'd better get a move on,' said Ditherus. The flames under their feet were growing higher.

'I could show you Viscus in cell V,' Odium suggested. 'Apart from the limp he's fine.'

Gutsius shook his head. 'No use. I need them young and healthy.'

'What about the barbarian, then? Nasty temper

but strong as an ox.' Odium pointed at Bladderax, who seemed to be trying to put out the flames by roaring at them.

Gutsius went closer to get a better look. The barbarian was just what he was looking for – big, brutal and probably brainless. All the same he didn't want to pay too high a price, so he spat on the ground.

'Not what I'm after. Too flabby.'

'Flabby? That's pure muscle!' said Odium. 'Anyway, you could cut down his meals. Save money.'

'Yes, but barbarians are always trouble.'

Odium fingered the spot on his chin.

What about us? thought Ditherus. *What's wrong with us?* A drop of sweat ran down his nose, hung for a moment and plopped into the flames with a hiss. The soles of his feet felt like they were on fire. Maybe they *were* on fire. Tidio was running through the names of all the gods.

'Jupiter, save us, Mars, save us, Minerva, save us …'

'Not much I can offer you,' admitted Odium. 'They're all old or diseased except the skinny pair that came in yesterday.'

Ditherus looked up.

'Not much to look at, I grant you,' said Odium, 'but I could let you have 'em cut-price. Don't tell Marcus Furius, though, he wants them dead.'

Gutsius walked over to inspect them. Ditherus tried to puff out his chest – but the smoke made him cough. Gutsius shook his head.

'Skin and bone. I need MEN, not BOYS!'

'Give us a chance!' croaked Ditherus.

'What did he say?' asked Gutsius.

'He says they can dance.'

'I'm not running a circus,' snorted Gutsius, turning his attention back to Bladderax.

'If there's nothing else, I'll take the barbarian. I could take him off your hands for, say – three denarii. I'd be doing you a favour.'

'Three? It's robbery!' protested Odium.

'ARRGHH!' roared Bladderax. 'I HOT FEET!'

'Four, then. Make up your mind or he'll be overcooked.'

'Ten,' said Odium. 'I couldn't take any less.'

The bargaining continued. Ditherus let his head loll forwards in despair. The flames crackled in his ears. *So this is the end*, he thought. He'd never know whether one day he might have become a hero.

'Goodbye, Tidio,' he wheezed.

'Five,' boomed Gutsius. 'It's my last offer.'

'Make it six and I'll throw in the two shrimps free of charge.'

Gutsius laughed. 'I must be going soft. All right, six; it's a bargain.'

The two men spat on their hands and shook on the agreement. They might have gone on chatting for a while if a roar from Bladderax hadn't got their attention.

'ARGHHH! I BURNING TO SAUSAGE!'

A moment later there was a loud splash and clouds of smoke rose into the air, as the jailer doused the fire with buckets of water. The next bucket struck Ditherus full in the face and Odium grinned at him. 'Well!' he said. 'Looks like your lucky day!'

Some hours later, Ditherus and Tidio sat in the back of a cart as it bumped and shuddered down a stony road. Their companions were sullen, scowling men with chains round their ankles. Ditherus had managed to rescue the Nemesis from his cell and kept it hidden inside his tunic. Tidio, meanwhile, was examining the blisters on the soles of his feet.

At last they came in sight of a grim building that resembled an army barracks surrounded by high walls. Two heavy wooden gates creaked open to let them through. Someone had scrawled on the wall, WELCOME TO HADES. And a little further down: ENJOY YOUR STAY.

'What is this place?' Ditherus asked, as the gates slammed shut with a roll of thunder.

Gutsius glanced round from the driver's seat. 'This, boy? Didn't they tell you? This is Gladiator School.'

Chapter 6

School for Gladiators

The sun beat down. Ditherus did his best to try and listen to what Gutsius was saying. He hadn't slept much the previous night. For one thing he was sharing a bunk with Tidio, for another his fellow recruits snored like a herd of warthogs.

Now he stood in the hot, dusty practice ground with the other trainees, clutching his wooden sword and shield and wondering how he was going to survive the morning. Gutsius leaned on a stick with a knobbly head and surveyed his class. When he spoke his voice bounced off the walls all round them. He had a habit of bellowing out words to make sure no one dozed off to sleep.

'So which of you WEAKLINGS think you know how to FIGHT?' he boomed.

Most of the recruits slowly raised their hands.

Gutsius spat in the dust contemptuously. 'Babies! Infants! Look at you!'

Ditherus glanced at his companions. They didn't look like infants; most of them looked like they had criminal records.

'YOU!' roared Gutsius, pointing to a tall, hook-nosed man. 'OUT THE FRONT!'

The man came out, gripping his sword and shield a little nervously.

'Knock me down,' Gutsius invited. 'GO ON! A big OAF like you! Show me how it's done!'

The tall recruit gripped his wooden sword and aimed a blow at the gladiator master's head. The stick in Gutsius's hand swished through the air. The knobbly end caught the man on the side of the head and dumped him on the ground.

'ANYONE ELSE LIKE TO TRY?' asked

Gutsius. A single hand was raised in the air. It belonged to Bladderax. The big barbarian barged his way through the crowd to the front. Gutsius peered up at the red-haired giant towering over him and cleared his throat.

'Uh . . . what was your name again?'

'I Bladderax.'

'Good, excellent. Glad to see you're paying attention,' blustered Gutsius. 'Back to your place, then, and keep up the good work.'

He turned back to his audience and continued his welcome speech.

'Three days,' he said. 'In three days I'll be sending you knock-kneed, spineless WHELKS into the ARENA! Where people – Mars help us! – will be paying good MONEY to see you FIGHT!' He paused to wipe some sweat off his bald, glistening head. 'SO every day from dawn to dusk we are going to be TRAINING HARD! I'm going to take you simpering MUMMY'S BOYS and turn you into GLADIATORS. INTO WHAT?

'GLADIATORS, MASTER!' the recruits shouted back.

'YOU! Why are you waving your hand?' demanded Gutsius.

'Please, sir, may I go to the toilet?' asked a voice at the back.

Gutsius raised his eyes to heaven.

They began the first lesson – *training at the post*. Ditherus was relieved to see his first opponent was made of wood. Sunk into the ground were a dozen round posts, and for the next hour the trainees performed a strange dance around them. Ditherus practised bobbing and weaving. He learned to lunge, point and leap backwards. His sword made satisfying swishing noises through the air, while Gutsius strode among them barking orders.

'Thrust! Don't pat it like a BABY'S BOTTOM! This is your ENEMY – he's trying to KILL YOU! Ludicrus, you dozy pimple, the POINTY bit does the stabbing! For the love of Mars put your BACK into it!'

Ditherus felt he was making progress. He landed quite a number of good thwacks and jabs. Tidio, meanwhile, had lost his sword in some bushes and seemed to be taking his time finding it.

'You! Chicken legs! Don't just DAB at it! Where are you AIMING?'

Ditherus realised Gutsius was talking to him.

'Um, I don't know. At his tummy?' he suggested.

'His TUMMY, you MISERABLE MOLLUSC?'

The recruits roared with laughter. Ditherus felt his cheeks burning red.

'You STRIKE where he's not protected by armour.

That's HEAD! CHEST! ARMS! LEGS!' Gutsius thwacked these areas on the wooden pole with his stick. 'Show me, boy. ATTACK!'

Ditherus shuffled forward, gave the post a quick poke with his sword and sprang back as if it might bite him.

'YE GODS, BOY!' roared Gutsius. 'Not like that! BLADDERAX, you show him!'

Bladderax stepped forward. With a bloodcurdling roar he rushed at one of the posts, slashing and hacking at it like a madman so that lumps of splintered wood shot off in all directions. He dealt the post a final death blow that made it shudder, and stepped back, breathing heavily.

'Not bad,' said Gutsius. 'Now you, chicken legs. Show me.'

'Yaaah!' Ditherus cried, waving his wooden sword with such gusto that it slipped right out of his hand.

Gutsius picked it up from the dust. 'NO, YOU LUGWORM! It's a BATTLECRY, you're not playing peek-a-boo with your baby sister! Put some FEELING into it!'

Ditherus screwed his face into a ball and

narrowed his eyes, which was probably a mistake since his eyesight wasn't that good. He launched himself like a missile.

'RARRRRRRGH!'

Something hard rose up and struck him between the eyes. It was the training post, and he slid to the ground.

The other recruits sniggered and shook their heads.

'Think it's FUNNY, DO YOU?' Gutsius turned on them. 'Think you can do BETTER? Good, then let's see how you do against REAL GLADIATORS!'

The sniggers died away. Up to now the class had been kept well away from the seasoned gladiators at the school, but they had all heard thumps and shouts coming from over the wall. Now Gutsius marched over to a door and banged on it three times with his stick.

The door swung open and through it came the ugliest, meanest warriors that Ditherus had ever seen. They were bare-chested, with muscles bulging like bags of bananas. Some had shaven heads and sported impressive tattoos. Skulls, dragons and sea serpents grinned from their arms and shoulders. Several seemed to have lost a few things – such as ears, fingers or teeth. Their swords, daggers and pointed tridents gleamed wickedly in the sun. Just looking at them gave Ditherus a strong urge to run in the opposite direction.

Gutsius's eyes twinkled. 'Right, my young lions, everyone find a PARTNER and let's begin!'

Ditherus was paired with a handsome gladiator called Silvio. Luckily he seemed more interested in talking than fighting.

'So,' he said, tossing back his long golden hair and flashing his perfect teeth, 'I can see you're thinking "Is it really him?"'

'Not really,' said Ditherus.

'It's OK, I get it all the time.'

'Get what?

'People staring. Recognising me.'

'But I don't,' said Ditherus.

'Nonsense! You do! I'm Silvio. Silvio the Great.'

'Sorry,' shrugged Ditherus. 'Never heard of you.'

Silvio stared in disbelief. 'Don't drag your sword,' he advised. 'Point it like this. And try to copy me.'

Ditherus did his best. Silvio was bobbing around like a rabbit but he never came close enough to actually land a blow.

'Aren't you a bit on the small side for a gladiator?' he asked.

Ditherus rolled his eyes. People were always saying things like this. 'I didn't exactly volunteer. This was sort of an accident,' he replied.

'You'll get used to it,' said Silvio. 'It's not a bad

life. Fresh air, three meals a day. If you're lucky, one day you might be as famous as me. Are you *sure* you haven't heard of me?'

'Positive,' replied Ditherus.

'What about those bronze coins you can collect: "Gladiators of the Golden Age"? Surely you must have seen them? I'm Number XXV.'

'Look,' said Ditherus, growing tired of this. 'Aren't we meant to be fighting?'

'That's what we're *doing*,' shouted Silvio. 'It's all about timing! I'm like a cobra poised to *strike*.'

He performed a neat pirouette and lunged with his sword, which Ditherus easily swatted away with his shield. His head was still throbbing from running into the post, and he needed to sit down.

'Goat's milk,' winked Silvio.

'What?'

'My hair. I wash it in goat's milk. That's what gives it the shine.'

'That isn't what I wanted to know,' said Ditherus. 'When's our day off?'

Silvio threw back his head and laughed. 'Day off? Didn't they tell you? You're here till you die – which if you don't keep your shield up could be pretty soon.'

Ditherus was horrified. 'You mean we're never allowed out?'

'Never – apart from the Games. They give us cloaks for the parade, you know, trimmed with gold. You should hear the women screaming my name –'

'Yes, yes,' said Ditherus impatiently. 'But why doesn't anyone try to escape?'

Silvio waved his sword at the high walls. 'Look around you, this place is a fortress. The guards are on a bonus if they catch anyone trying to escape. Now do you mind if we get back to the point?'

'What point?' said Ditherus.

'Are you *sure* you haven't heard of me?'

Chapter 7

Never Voluteer

'You're sure you're all right?' Tidio asked as they waited in the queue for lunch.

'Stop fussing, will you? It's just a graze,' said Ditherus.

'There's a lump on your head the size of an egg.'

Ditherus felt his forehead gingerly. He still had a throbbing headache but it was his pride that really hurt. In front of the whole school he'd fought a wooden post and lost.

'Still, I think you made a dent in it,' Tidio grinned. 'It could be a new way of fighting. The flying headbutt.'

They were almost at the front of the queue, where a slave in a filthy apron was ladling out a mess of stew. Ditherus felt a heavy hand on his shoulder and turned to see their former cellmate, Bladderax.

'You push in. This MY place,' snarled the barbarian.

'No we didn't,' said Ditherus. 'We were in front of you.'

'You in Bladderax place. MOVE!' bellowed Bladderax, giving Ditherus a shove that almost knocked him off his feet. Ditherus was about to argue but Tidio grabbed him by the arm.

'Leave him, master!'

'Did you see that? He pushed me!' grumbled Ditherus.

'He's a barbarian, master, manners aren't their strong point.'

Ditherus scowled at Bladderax's massive back. 'I have to start standing up for myself some time,' he muttered.

*

They took their bowls of watery bean stew and sat down in the shade of a tree to eat.

'Master, might I suggest we leave as soon as possible,' said Tidio.

'Don't worry about me, Tidio, I think I'm starting to get the hang of it,' replied Ditherus. 'Anyway, we're safer here than in prison.'

'Safer?' said Tidio. 'In three days' time you could be fighting in the arena – against someone like that!' He pointed to a gladiator sitting nearby with legs like tree trunks and a budding moustache. On a closer look, Ditherus realised it was a woman.

'Anyway,' Ditherus said. 'Aren't you forgetting something?'

'What?'

'I still have Brutalus's sword hidden under the mattress.'

'Even so, master, maybe you're not cut out to be a gladiator. Maybe you're a little . . .'

'What?' demanded Ditherus. 'Small? Weedy?'

'No, just a little . . . sensitive.'

Ditherus scowled – his mother was always saying he was sensitive. Just because he used to pass out every time he got a nosebleed. 'In any case,' he said, 'this place is a fortress. How are we going to escape?'

Tidio didn't have time to answer. The gladiatrix had stepped into the practice ring. It looked like lunchtime was over since Gutsius was shouting again.

'Gather round, I have a little TREAT for you! Some of our champion gladiators are going to show you how it's done. Anyone MAN enough can step into the ring and challenge them. So who'll fight VOLUPTA?'

There was a silence, broken only by Tidio slurping his stew.

'Step forward! Don't tell me you're scared of A WOMAN?' boomed Gutsius.

The recruits shuffled their feet and stared at the ground. None of them had any wish to fight a woman, especially one who looked like she might break them in half. Even Bladderax found he was suddenly interested in the state of his fingernails.

Gutsius struck the sand with his stick. 'One volunteer? I'M WAITING!'

At the back of the crowd, Ditherus rose to his knees to get a better view. Gutsius spotted him and pointed with his stick.

'You at the BACK! A boy with PLUCK, that's what I like to see!'

Ditherus blinked in alarm. 'Me? No, I wasn't . . .'

'Out here and stop BLEATING!' roared Gutsius. 'A HELMET for our brave challenger!'

Ditherus felt Tidio tug at his arm. 'Master,' Tidio whispered. 'She looks rather dangerous.'

Ditherus tried to ignore the way Volupta was pawing the sand like a bull about to charge.

'Don't worry. It's just a practice fight,' he said, try-

69

ing to sound more calm than he felt. 'She's not actually going to hurt me.'

'But has anyone told her that?' said Tidio.

Volupta bared her teeth, which were mostly black. The crowd closed in around the ring, eager not to miss anything.

Ditherus pulled on the heavy bronze helmet he'd been given. It was so big it kept slipping down so the eyeholes were level with his nose. He gripped his wooden training sword.

Gutsius was bellowing instructions. 'POINT your sword! Keep your SHIELD UP! Don't BACK OFF!'

Ditherus tried to obey but it was hard to concentrate on three things at once. He tried to recall what the books said about defending yourself. Attack was the best form of defence or was it the other way round?

Volupta advanced.

'Move your feet!' advised Silvio's voice from the crowd. Ditherus bobbed and weaved, keeping well out of Volupta's reach.

'For the love of Mars, stop PRANCING AROUND!' roared Gutsius. 'ATTACK her!'

Ditherus made a rush at his enemy and lunged with his wooden sword. The point prodded Volupta's iron stomach. She didn't flinch. Ditherus heard a loud crack as Volupta plucked it from his hand and snapped it clean in half. He gulped. Tidio closed his eyes, unable to watch. Ditherus's helmet had slipped down so far he didn't even see the blow coming – but he felt it crash down on his head with the force of a sledgehammer.

'OOOOOOOH!' went the watching crowd.

He took a step backwards before his legs buckled and he sank to the ground. Cheers echoed in his ears. Someone pulled off his battered helmet and Gutsius's bald head swam into view.

'Still ALIVE, chicken legs?'

Ditherus nodded weakly. 'Did I win?'

'Not exactly. Fifty-eight seconds, that could be a record. Still you showed SPIRIT, I'll give you that.'

Chapter 8

Pass the Bull's Blood

Two nights later, long tables were set out in the courtyard for the Feast of Heroes. The feast was always held the night before the Games and generously provided by Porcus Maximus IV. It was also a good way for the school to make some easy money. Gutsius had been selling tickets all day and crowds of curious sightseers were already gathering to watch.

The tables groaned under the weight of all the

food. Ditherus stared gloomily at the plates piled high with pigs' trotters, calves' livers, sheep's eyes, ox tongues and hogs' bottoms. Somehow knowing this might be his last meal on earth spoiled his appetite.

Huge jugs of bull's blood wine were passed round and by the time Gutsius rose to his feet, it had gone to a few heads. Bladderax and Omnibus were arm-wrestling across the table, while Ludicrus was face down with his head in a bowl of stew. Gutsius's fist thumped down on the table, catapulting a plate of snails high into the air.

'MEN, BROTHERS, FELLOW GLADIA-TORS,' he roared, 'GREAT NEWS! Our Noble Emperor, Porcus Maximus, has declared that the Games will be held in honour of our glorious vic-tory in Gaul. TOMORROW AT NOON WE FIGHT!'

The gladiators whooped, pumped their fists, and slapped each other on the back as if they'd just won the lotterium. Even Bladderax stopped crushing his opponent's fingers to listen. Ditherus's mind was racing. If the war was over, maybe his dad was at last on his way home?

'When you go out into the arena walk out with

pride,' Gutsius went on, addressing the rows of eager, excited faces. 'Remember the motto of our school – *Nullus Amat Snivellum* – No one likes a crybaby. I don't want anyone FAINTING or asking to go to the TOILET. Fight like Romans and die like men. I raise my cup to you – DO OR DIE!'

'DO OR DIE!' the men chorused, echoing the age-old battle cry of gladiators.

'But probably die,' muttered Ditherus to himself.

Gutsius drained his cup to the dregs and tossed it aside.

'Now to the moment you've been waiting for,' he roared. 'The ROLL OF HONOUR.'

He pulled a scroll from his pocket and began to unroll it. 'As well as the usual man-eating lions, there will be THIRTY COMBATS. Which means LUCKILY some of you NEW BOYS will get your moment of glory.'

'Oh, hooray,' groaned Ditherus as he was deafened by cheering. By this point the gladiators would have cheered if Gutsius had ordered them to jump in a pit of scorpions.

Tidio raised his hand. He was serving at tables tonight as Gutsius had decided he would never make a gladiator.

'Yes?' growled Gutsius.

'Just a question, master. What if someone felt they'd rather not fight?' asked Tidio.

Gutsius's face went dark as thunder. 'RATHER – NOT – FIGHT?' he choked.

'Yes, I mean if someone felt they weren't . . . quite ready . . .' Tidio's words trailed away.

Ditherus guessed he was talking about him. But excuses were useless.

Gutsius barged his way through the crowd and

seized him by the throat. 'If I say they will FIGHT, you snivelling jug-eared JELLYFISH, they will go out and FIGHT! Do I make myself CLEAR?'

'Crystal clear, master,' croaked Tidio.

Gutsius released him. 'Now where was I?'

'The Roll of Honour,' prompted Silvio.

Gutsius began to read out the roll, which listed the names of those chosen to fight in the Games.

'First round combats – SCABIUS will fight BEEFCAKE, SILVIO will fight OMNIBUS ...'

The list went on, with the audience cheering every name. Ditherus listened with his heart pounding. He'd always dreamed of fighting in the *Colosseum*[4], but now he wasn't so sure he was ready. Mercifully the list was nearing the end and his name didn't seem to be on it.

'Bladderax the Barbarian . . .' boomed Gutsius and paused for dramatic effect, '... will fight DITHERUS.'

Loud cheers and hoots of laughter greeted this announcement. Ditherus looked at Bladderax oppo-

---

4 **Colosseum** – nickname of the great Roman amphitheatre where the Games were held.

site him, who was smiling wolfishly. The big barbarian leaned forward, scooped up a sheep's eyeball from a bowl and held it in the palm of his hand.

'I kill you good,' he leered. 'Plenty blood. I squish you like flea.'

His fingers closed over the sheep's eye and squeezed. There was a loud pop as it exploded. Ditherus felt he was going to be sick.

Chapter 9

Time to Escape

As the feast went on into the night, Ditherus sank deeper and deeper into gloom. Bladderax of all people – why did it have to be him? The giant barbarian was already heavy-weight arm-wrestling champion of the entire school.

His thoughts were interrupted by Tidio's hand on his shoulder.

'Don't look so worried, master,' he said, speaking softly. 'Tonight we make our escape. And the gods are with us – look over there.'

Ditherus looked behind him and to his amazement spotted his mother among the rows of spectators. When no one was looking he slipped over to see her.

'Ditherus darling!' Hilaria exclaimed in surprise. 'What *on earth* are you doing here?'

Ditherus wished she would keep her voice down – right now he didn't want to attract attention.

'There isn't time to explain, Mum,' he said. 'I need your help.'

Hilaria sighed. 'Well, of course, pumpkin, but I do wish you'd tell me what's going on. First you run off to prison, then you turn up here. And what have you done with your clothes?'

Ditherus looked at what he was wearing, which wasn't much more than a loincloth.

'Mum, I'm a gladiator,' he explained. 'I'm fighting in the Games tomorrow.'

Hilaria threw back her head and laughed.

'What's so funny?' asked Ditherus.

'Well, you are, cupcake. Gladiators are big muscly fellows. You can't just *become* one, it takes months of practice.'

'Mum, that's why I'm here. It's a gladiator school.'

'Well, I know that, darling. I must say that fair-haired one is quite good-looking . . .'

Ditherus could see it was going to be one of those conversations that might go on a long time. 'Please,' he said. 'You've got to help us get out of here or tomorrow I'm probably going to be chopped into mincemeat.'

'Well, of course I'll help, poppet.' Hilaria smiled, ruffling his hair fondly. 'But I can't see why you're making such a fuss. I'll just tell them I'm your mum and I'm taking you home.'

Hilaria rose from her seat and Ditherus quickly pulled her back down. 'No, Mum! It's not that easy. We're not allowed out – there are guards watching the gate. We have to escape without being seen.'

'Escape? Goodness, how exciting!' said Hilaria, pressing his hand and giggling. Ditherus closed his eyes. This was never going to work.

Some of the spectators were starting to leave and he could see Gutsius at the gate, checking everyone who went out.

'Anyway, pumpkin, it will be nice to have you

home,' Hilaria was saying. 'You've no idea what a *dreadful* time I've been having.'

'Really?' said Ditherus, hardly listening.

'Quite awful, darling. Ever since all this fuss about you stealing the Emperor's sword . . .'

'I didn't STEAL IT,' sighed Ditherus.

'Well, borrowed it, then. Ever since then I have the feeling everyone's avoiding me. And all because of these silly rumours.'

'What rumours?' asked Ditherus.

'Well, you know, that your father is plotting to become emperor.'

Ditherus stared at her. 'Dad? That's ridiculous!'

'That's what *I* said, darling. He'd make a terrible emperor! You know how he hates dinner parties!'

Ditherus frowned. Tidio had been right all along. Someone was behind all this and there was only one person it could be. 'It's Marcus Furius,' he said grimly. 'First he had me thrown in prison and now he's out to get Dad in trouble. We've got to stop him!'

Tidio came over to join them. 'We need to hurry,' he said. 'If we join the crowd now, maybe we can slip through the gates unseen.'

Ditherus shook his head. 'Gutsius is watching. We'll never get past him.'

Tidio looked thoughtfully at Hilaria. 'Mistress, forgive me, but may I borrow your cloak?'

'Certainly not,' said Hilaria. 'It's new.'

'Please, it's only for a moment.' Tidio took the light blue cloak and draped it over Ditherus's head, wrapping it round his face so that only his eyes and nose were visible. 'There,' he said, standing back to admire his handiwork.

'Actually, pigeon, you do look rather sweet,' said Hilaria. 'The blue matches your eyes.'

Ditherus scowled. 'I'm not wearing this. I look like a girl!'

'Exactly, master, so no one will suspect you,' said Tidio. 'Keep your head down and it just might work.'

They joined the large crowd which was now edging slowly towards the gate. Keeping a firm grip on his mother's arm, Ditherus tried to steer her into the middle of the throng. Tidio kept close behind them with his head bowed low. A few more seconds and they would be level with the gate. Ditherus had to shuffle along taking small steps as his ankles were chained together like all the other gladiators. The chain dragged along the ground, clinking whenever it hit a rock. He prayed that Gutsius wouldn't look down as they passed.

Just as they reached the gate, a gap opened up in the crowd ahead of them and Gutsius stepped out in front of them. Ditherus resisted the urge to run.

'Ladies!' said Gutsius, bowing low.

To Ditherus's horror, Hilaria stopped as if she

wanted to strike up a conversation. 'Thank you, a most interesting evening,' she said, dropping a few coins into the gladiator master's hand.

'And this must be your daughter?' asked Gutsius, looking at Ditherus.

'Daughter?' said Hilaria, frowning. Ditherus pinched her arm. 'Ow! Yes, of course, my daughter. This is Dizzius . . . Diana!'

'Charmed to meet you, mistress,' said the gladiator master with a wink. Ditherus was alarmed to see Gutsius smiling at him in a roguish sort of way. If they hung around much longer, he'd be asking for a kiss. He pulled his cloak up higher and tried a girlish laugh, which came out like a nervous squawk.

'Well, we must be going, goodnight!' said Hilaria.

They walked on quickly. A few more paces and they were past the guards and passing through the gate. Ditherus could feel Gutsius's eyes following him and couldn't help glancing back. The gladiator master was staring after them with a puzzled expression. His eyes were fixed on Ditherus's ankles and the heavy chain dragging between them. Slowly the truth dawned on his face and he let out a roar of fury.

'RUN!' yelped Ditherus. There were shouts behind them as the three of them broke into an ungainly run. They might have escaped, but running with your ankles chained together is like trying to run in a three-legged race. Eventually you are bound to stumble or fall over. Ditherus fell over. The next moment hands pulled him roughly to his feet and the cloak was torn from his head.

'So, chicken legs,' growled Gutsius. 'Not planning on LEAVING US, were you?'

Chapter 10

Enter the Gladiators

Ditherus stood in the shadow of the massive Gate of Life, waiting his turn to go on. Through a crack he could glimpse the arena and the faces of the crowd. In the tunnel behind him several of the other gladiators were limbering up. Some of them were doing stretches while Silvio danced around, practising his footwork. Personally Ditherus felt if he jumped about too much he might be sick. His stomach felt like a volcano about to erupt.

86

Bladderax was the only one who looked relaxed. He was amusing himself skewering passing flies on the point of his sword. It was easily the biggest sword Ditherus had ever seen – a Titan Thunderbolt with a curved blade that looked wickedly sharp. The barbarian swung it around as if it was as light as a cucumber. (Ditherus wouldn't have minded fighting someone armed with a cucumber.) In honour of the Games, Bladderax had daubed his face and chest with blue woad. His mane of red hair was braided into plaits which gave him the look of a Viking raider. Below the waist he wore a tartan kilt held up by a wide leather belt with a skull's-head buckle. Ditherus looked down at his own skinny frame and wondered where he was when the gods were handing out muscles. He was sweating now, partly due to the heat but mostly because he was about to fight a mad barbarian armed with a meat cleaver. He wished Tidio was here to calm his nerves.

High above the ring, Porcus Maximus IV lay back on a mound of cushions and waited for the next fight to begin. His only duties at the Games were eating and waving – both things which he did superbly well.

Occasionally he had to decide the fate of a gladiator by giving a thumbs-up or thumbs-down – but luckily he could do that without having to get up.

Sitting next to him, Marcus Furius leaned in closer to speak.

'I've been thinking, Your Excellency . . .'

'Really?' yawned Porcus. 'Thinking always gives me a headache.'

'Yes, Majesty, but I was thinking about Caius Wart,' said Furius.

'Wart?' The Emperor glanced idly at his programme. 'Is he fighting today?'

'No, Majesty. Caius Wart, general of your army.'

'Ah yes, Caius, splendid fellow. I gather he beat those girls in the end.' Porcus paused to help himself to a plate of larks' tongues.

'Gauls, Excellency, yes. I'm told the army is on its way home now.'

'Good, then we'll have a victory parade. I'm very fond of parades. I could ride through the streets in my chariot, so people can cheer me. And we'll throw a banquet for Caius. You know, conquering hero, that kind of thing.'

Furius's face darkened. 'You are too generous,

Majesty, but aren't you forgetting something?'

'What? A chariot's too small? You think I'd look better on an elephant?'

'No, I meant you're forgetting that Wart is a traitor. Surely you've heard the rumours?'

'Rumours?' said Porcus.

'That Wart is plotting to have you . . . *removed*.' Furius drew a finger slowly across his throat.

The Emperor turned pale. 'You're not serious?'

'I'm afraid so, Your Trembliness.'

'But surely not Caius, he's always been so loyal!'

Furius shook his head. 'Sadly, Majesty, the facts are only too plain. Remember last week his own son tried to attack you?'

'Heavens yes!'

'If I hadn't been there, I dread to think what might have happened.'

'Quite,' said Porcus. 'I might have been killed! Murdered even.'

'Exactly, Highness, but there's something that worries me more.'

'More? Oh dear!'

'Caius is returning to Rome with an army of ten

thousand at his command.' Furius gave the Emperor a long, meaningful look.

'Is that bad?' asked Porcus.

'Very bad, Excellency. If he is plotting to have you *removed*.'

'Oh by the gods!' spluttered Porcus. 'If Caius has an army . . .'

'Yes indeed, Your Anxiousness.'

'He might try to . . .'

'I fear so.'

'Marcus, this is terrible! What am I going to do?'

This was the question Furius had been waiting for. He thumped his fist on the table. 'CRUSH THE TRAITOR!' he said. 'Have him arrested, thrown in prison.'

'But he's our best general! If I have him arrested, who's going to lead the army?'

Furius leaned in to speak in Porcus's ear. 'Majesty, replace Wart with someone you can trust. Someone close to you.'

Porcus frowned. 'You mean . . . my wife?'

'NO!' roared Furius, losing patience. 'I mean ME! ME!'

'Well, all right, there's no need to shout,' said Porcus.

Furius released the Emperor's toga, which he seemed to have grabbed in his excitement. 'Then you promise, Your Worthiness, I will be general?'

Porcus was about to answer but he was distracted by a movement below. 'Oh, look, the gates are opening!' he pointed. 'The next fight's about to start.'

Marcus Furius watched as the slaves cleared the arena. It was in his grasp now. Wart would be disgraced, branded a traitor, finally out of his way – and then nothing could stop him.

Down below, Ditherus watched as the gates swung back. Tidio and another slave came hurrying through the gates, dragging a body between them. Ditherus didn't go too close but it looked like Silvio the Great. He swallowed hard.

'You're on next, master. Are you all right?' said Tidio, coming over.

Ditherus nodded. 'A little nervous. Well, a lot nervous really.'

Tidio glanced across at Bladderax, who was waiting impatiently to be called. 'Just try to keep out of his reach,' he advised. 'The first time he swings, go down and ask the Emperor for mercy.'

'Isn't that cheating?' Ditherus frowned. 'I'm supposed to fight him.'

'Master, it's your only chance. Maybe the crowd will take pity on you.'

'Right. Thanks for the vote of confidence,' said Ditherus.

The trumpets blew a long blast, calling them to the arena. Ditherus took a deep breath.

'Well, good luck, master,' said Tidio. 'Sorry I can't stay.'

'You're not going to watch?'

Tidio shook his head. 'I wish I could, master, but Marcus Furius is with the Emperor. I think there may be a way to make him confess.'

'Really? How?' said Ditherus.

'There isn't time to explain. If all goes well, I'll meet you back here. Just pray your mother remembers what to do.'

'My mother?' said Ditherus. 'What's she got to do with it? Is she here?'

'Of course, master. She never misses the Games. She should be on her way to the Imperial Box now.'

'Why?' asked Ditherus.

'To speak to Furius.'

Tidio hugged him for a last time. 'I'll explain later. The gods protect you, master. You have the sword?'

Ditherus touched the Nemesis at his belt. 'Maybe the legend is true,' he said hopefully. 'As long as I have this nothing can hurt me. I'm invincible.'

'Maybe,' said Tidio. 'That's the trouble with legends, you never really know.' He hurried away, jangling a bunch of keys which Ditherus could have sworn belonged on Gutsius's belt.

Ditherus had no idea what Tidio was planning, but any scheme that involved his mother was bound to go wrong. In any case, right now he had enough worries of his own. Pulling on his helmet, he began to walk what seemed like a hundred miles to the centre of the arena, where Bladderax was waiting.

His entrance was greeted with stunned silence. In the Imperial Box, Porcus Maximus checked his programme to see if this was the comedy part with the clowns. The pint-size gladiator who had just entered

the ring wore a wobbly helmet and held an ancient sword which looked oddly familiar.

'At least we'll see some blood now,' remarked Marcus Furius. So far the fights had been disappointing – one gladiator had sprained his ankle, one had trodden on his own trident, and two had collapsed with sunstroke. Furius had attended funerals more exciting than this.

Someone tapped him on the shoulder and he turned round to see Hilaria, smiling at him in an odd way.

'Marcus!' she gushed. 'How lovely to see you! Would you care for a walk?'

A few minutes later they were following one of the dark passageways that led under the arena.

'How much further?' asked Furius.

'Oh, not far now,' replied Hilaria, who wasn't exactly sure they were going the right way. Tidio's instructions were to bring Furius to the animal cells by the west gate. But which way was west? Like right and left it was easy to get muddled. At first Furius had been reluctant to come, but Hilaria had cleverly invented a beautiful sister who was dying to meet him. Men were always interested in your beautiful sister.

'You haven't told me her name,' said Furius.

'Oh, her name . . .' Hilaria hadn't actually thought of a name. 'She's called . . . um . . . Vanilla! Yes, she talks about you all the time.'

'Really?' Furius halted. He was finding this all a bit hard to believe. He'd never had much success with women. Things started off all right until he shouted or gave them an order, then they suddenly remembered they had to be somewhere else. 'So what does she look like?' he asked.

'Well . . . ah . . . a bit like me,' replied Hilaria.

'Oh,' said Marcus Furius, looking as if he wanted to turn back.

Hilaria resisted the urge to poke him in the eye. 'Well, obviously younger and more beautiful than me,' she said. 'And she admires you tremendously.'

'Really? What about me?' Furius had actually gone a little pink.

'Oh, well, she loves your um . . .' Hilaria struggled to find something attractive about Furius. It wasn't easy. He had blazing eyes, a cruel mouth and the face of an angry bulldog. 'Your ears,' said Hilaria.

'She loves my EARS?'

'Adores them. The way they stick out on either side of your head. And the shape of them – like little pink seashells. She says she could gaze at your ears all day.'

Furius blinked in amazement. 'But if she likes me so much why haven't we met?'

'Oh, well, because . . . she's so shy. Look, here we are at last!' said Hilaria, with great relief.

Marcus Furius looked around. They were in a dingy passageway with a horrible smell. It didn't seem a very romantic place to meet. A slave was jangling some keys, unlocking a door to one of the cells. Judging from the roars and boos above them, they were close to the arena.

'So where is she?' demanded Furius.

'Ah yes, where?' Hilaria looked at Tidio for help. He jerked his head towards the cell. Hilaria stared at him blankly. He rolled his eyes and pointed several times to the door. Still Hilaria looked blank.

'Oh, this is ridiculous, I'm going back,' snapped Furius.

Tidio groaned and grabbed him by the arm, dragging him back to the cell.

'Oh, I see! In there!' cried Hilaria, grasping it at long last.

Marcus Furius peered through the barred door. 'Are you sure? It's pitch-dark.'

'Well, I told you she's shy,' said Hilaria.

Furius stepped inside the door. The scent was stronger here, almost animal, but then women these days wore all kinds of strange perfume.

'Why don't you call her?' suggested Hilaria.

'Vanilla? It's me, Marcus!' cooed Furius. 'Don't be shy, my dove!'

A long, low growl came back in reply.

Furius stepped back. 'Great gods! What was that?'

'I think she's calling you,' suggested Tidio.

'Is she?' said Furius.

'Absolutely,' said Hilaria. 'I'd know her voice anywhere. Well go on, don't keep her waiting.'

Furius went further into the cell, wishing he'd brought a candle. The floor was covered in filthy straw. At the far end someone – or something – was stirring in the darkness. Suddenly the cell door clanged shut, making him jump. He swung round, sensing too late that this was a trick.

'Hey, you! Slave! Open the door!'

Tidio turned the key in the lock and slipped it into his pocket. 'That depends,' he said, 'on whether you're ready to talk.'

The hairs stood up on the back of Furius's neck.

Something was moving, coming towards him. Something large that padded on all fours. 'Vanilla?' he quavered. 'Is that you . . . dear?'

Very slowly he turned round and let out a whimper. The lion was looking straight at him – and it wasn't admiring his ears.

Chapter 11

Fighting Bladderax

Back in the arena, Ditherus tried to remember what he'd read. *Look your opponent in the eyes* – advice that didn't help much when your enemy was seven foot tall. Bladderax did some impressive sword twirling and hurled his Titan Thunderbolt into the air, catching it one-handed. The crowd gasped in admiration. Ditherus tried a few wild swishes of his Nemesis and dropped it in the sand. Jeers and laughter rang out. Bladderax threw back his head and roared the barbarian battle cry, which woke up several spectators in the back row. He lumbered forward, eager to get on with it.

'*Run!*' urged a voice in Ditherus's head. He wanted to run but his legs seemed to have forgotten how to do it. Instead he crouched behind his shield, as Bladderax bore down on him. '*Move your feet. Keep your shield up. He's just as scared as you are,*' Ditherus muttered to himself.

The first sweep of the Thunderbolt sliced the plume off his helmet. The second smashed into his shield. By some miracle he met the third with a clash of steel on steel. *This is great*, he thought, *I'm actually fighting. Like a real gladiator*. It was as if the Nemesis knew where it wanted to go. Just as he was marvelling at this, the next blow battered his helmet and knocked him right off his feet.

'OOOH!' cried the crowd.

Porcus Maximus clapped his hands. This was more like it. Next to an even fight there was nothing he liked better than a merciless slaughter.

'What a pity Marcus isn't here to see this,' he said.

'Yes,' agreed Hilaria, who'd just sat down. 'I think

he's a little busy right now.' She craned her neck for a better view of the skinny gladiator getting to his feet. There was something faintly familiar about him.

Bladderax had both arms raised in triumph. Some of the women in the upper tier were waving their hankies at him. He twirled a pigtail round his finger and waved back. Ditherus saw his chance. Running, he launched himself and leapt on to his opponent's back. Bladderax bellowed like an angry bull and swung him round, trying to shake him off. Ditherus was getting dizzy, losing his grip. The next moment he was flying through the air and hit the ground in a cloud of dust.

His eyes blinked open. The world was still spinning round. His hand groped for his sword, but it lay in the sand, just out of reach. An ugly, blue face peered down from the sky.

'Now I kill you good,' grunted Bladderax, raising his Titan Thunderbolt above his head.

A second later Ditherus would have been split in half like a pea. Luckily, he rolled to one side just as the Thunderbolt came down. He snatched up his Nemesis and slashed wildly at his opponent's belly.

He missed – but not altogether. Bladderax's leather belt dropped to the sand, neatly sliced in two. The barbarian's mouth dropped open and he looked down. His tartan kilt had begun to droop, and was now sliding past his knees. The crowd gasped. Women in the balcony covered their children's eyes. 'Great gods!' cried Porcus Maximus. He'd always wondered what barbarians wore under their kilts and now he knew.

Blushing scarlet, Bladderax reached down to pull up his kilt. But those few seconds were all Ditherus

needed. The point of his sword pricked his enemy's throat. The fight was over and by a miracle, Ditherus had won.

Bladderax hung his head, his pigtails drooping. 'You beat Bladderax. Now you kill him dead,' he said miserably. 'Chop off his ears, chop off his necks.'

Ditherus shook his head. 'I don't want to chop off anything,' he said. 'Ask the Emperor for mercy.'

Bladderax scowled stubbornly. 'I barbarian. Not beg like dog.'

The crowd wanted blood; they had begun to chant 'Kill! Kill! Kill!'

In the Imperial Box Porcus Maximus beat his fist in time and joined in.

Hilaria tapped him lightly on the shoulder. 'Your Excellency, sorry to interrupt but I think they're waiting for you.'

'Oh yes, of course. I'm the Emperor, aren't I? Now is it thumbs-up or thumbs-down? I always get mixed up.'

'Up for mercy, down for death,' prompted Hilaria.

'Splendid, splendid!' Porcus held out his thumb and slowly turned it down.

Bladderax saw the signal and sunk to his knees, baring his neck. 'Now you kill,' he said. 'Split my throat.'

Ditherus had turned rather pale himself. He didn't wish to split anyone's throat; it sounded messy. Out of the blue an idea came to him. 'Listen,' he whispered. 'You'll have to pretend.'

Bladderax gazed up at him, puzzled. 'Who is pretend?'

'You know. *Act*,' hissed Ditherus. 'I pretend to stab you. You fall down dead. *Pretend!*'

Bladderax widened his eyes. There was no telling if he understood but there wasn't time to explain. The crowd were growing restless. Ditherus raised his sword and plunged it into the barbarian – or actually into the narrow gap under his armpit. Bladderax rolled his eyes upwards and toppled to the ground dramatically.

'URGHHHHHHHHHH!' he gurgled.

Ditherus pulled out his sword. But Bladderax hadn't finished dying yet.

'Arggghhhhh! OOOHHHH! URRRKK! he moaned, rolling over and clutching at his belly.

'All right, don't overdo it,' muttered Ditherus.

Bladderax twitched a leg in the air and finally lay still. Ditherus raised his sword, the trumpets sounded once more and the crowd roared their approval.

As the wooden gates drew back, Tidio came hurrying out to meet him. 'Master! Are you all right?'

Ditherus pulled off his helmet and grinned. 'I told you I was invincible! Now help me shift this great lump, before anyone notices he's still breathing.'

They took hold of the barbarian's legs and began to drag him across the sand, grunting with the effort.

Halfway to the gates, Bladderax opened one eye. 'I big lump. I walk,' he offered.

'For Mars' sake, shut up!' hissed Ditherus. 'You're meant to be dead!'

As soon as the gates closed behind them, Bladderax sprung to his feet and hugged Ditherus so tightly he could hardly breathe.

'You plenty good friend,' he burbled. 'Save Bladderax life. I sorry try to squish you like flea. Now I your slaves for ever.'

Ditherus struggled to free himself. 'That's OK,' he said, 'I already have one slave.'

'Have two slaves.' Bladderax pointed to himself and Tidio. 'Big one and piddly one.'

Ditherus turned back to Tidio. He'd just remembered something. 'What about Marcus Furius?' he asked. 'You haven't told me what happened. Where is he?'

Tidio glanced back at the arena. 'Don't worry,' he said. 'I think you'll be seeing him any moment now.'

Chapter 12

A Roaring Time

No sooner had Tidio spoken than a heavy iron gate at the far end of the arena was raised.

In the Imperial Box the Emperor clapped his hands. 'Ah, splendid, the lions!' he exclaimed. 'My favourite.'

Unexpectedly a man came flying out, running so fast that his feet almost scorched the sand. He was bare-headed, white-faced and his uniform hung in tatters. The Emperor gasped in amazement.

'Great gods! Isn't that Marcus Furius?'

Hilaria shielded her eyes against the sun. 'It does look like him, Majesty.'

'But he never said he was taking part. His name's not in the programme!'

'No, Highness. Perhaps he wanted to keep it a surprise.'

Down below them, Marcus Furius looked around in desperation. The lions had spilled out of their cell and were prowling after him. For the last ten minutes Furius had been fending them off with his sword but that had only sharpened their appetite. He looked up at the Imperial Box and waved his arms frantically.

'Look, he's waving to me!' cried Porcus, waving back. 'HELLO, MARCUS! I must say it's jolly brave of him taking on a pack of lions single-handed. They look like brutes to me!' He clapped his hands excitedly. 'Bravo, Marcus! BRAVO!'

Furius had given up signalling for help. He was now running like a madman towards the far gates, which were shut against him. Two of the lions also broke into a run and started to close on him. Furius reached the gates first and began to claw his way up like a demented squirrel.

'What in Hades is he doing now?' asked Porcus.

'I think he's trying to escape, Excellency,' replied Hilaria.

Porcus frowned. 'Isn't that a bit cowardly? I thought the idea was to stand and fight!'

Furius had somehow managed to haul himself halfway up the gate. He was now clinging on like a limpet with the hungry lions snarling and snapping below.

The crowd began to jeer and boo. Porcus Maximus, who had been cheering wildly a moment ago, joined in.

'BOO!' he jeered. 'Come on, Marcus! Fight like a man!'

Marcus Furius paid no attention to the noise, but he knew he couldn't hold on much longer. He hammered on the gate with his fist. 'Open up, you fools! I command you, OPEN UP!'

Unfortunately for him, the only people on the other side of the gate were Ditherus and Tidio, and they weren't in any hurry to help.

'First give us your solemn promise,' Tidio called back.

Furius groaned. It was that interfering slave again – the one who'd tricked him into the lions' cell in the first place. Why wouldn't the wretch leave him alone?

'I've told you,' he whimpered. 'I don't know what you're talking about!'

'Then we'll leave you to your friends,' Tidio replied.

'NO, WAIT!' yelled Furius. He glanced down at the lions below. They were pacing back and forth, waiting for him to fall like a ripe plum. The big one with the scarred nose was slobbering at the mouth. He had no choice. 'All right! I'll say whatever you want!'

'Swear,' said Tidio.

'On my honour as a Roman.'

'HA!' scoffed Tidio. 'Swear by something else.'

'All right. By all the gods, the sun and the moon . . . whatever you want!'

'. . . That you will tell the Emperor the truth.'

'YES!' moaned Furius. 'For pity's sake, I'm slipping!'

One of the lions leapt in the air and snapped at his feet, missing by a whisker. Furius yelped.

Tidio turned to Ditherus. 'What do you think, master? Can we trust him?'

Bladderax pushed his blue face between them. 'Him bad man. Make plenty big troubles for you?'

'Very big troubles,' agreed Ditherus. 'All the same, we can't just leave him to be eaten. The problem is, how are we going to get him out?'

Tidio had already thought of an answer to this. A few seconds later a large slab of raw steak was tossed over the gates into the arena. As the lions pounced and fought over it hungrily, the gates drew back for a few seconds. Marcus Furius came scrambling through the gap on all fours and lay in the dust, panting and exhausted.

Bladderax picked him up by the scruff of the neck as if he was a naughty puppy. 'You bad man,' he scolded. 'Come with Bladderax. We go speak big Sneezer now.'

'Sneezer?' croaked Furius, still trembling with fright.

Ditherus smiled. 'I think he means Caesar.'

Chapter 13

The Emperor's Prize-giving

With a deafening blast of trumpets, Porcus Maximus IV rode into the arena in a golden chariot drawn by six white horses. It wasn't a long walk from the gates but he liked to make a big entrance.

The victorious gladiators waited in line to receive a prize. Above them the giant arena canopy flapped in the breeze, shading them from the sun. At the far end of the line stood Ditherus, flanked by Tidio and Bladderax. The barbarian had one brawny arm clamped round Marcus Furius's neck in case he tried to escape. When it was finally his turn, Ditherus stepped forward and bowed.

'Ah, splendid, the brave little gladiator!' Porcus beamed.

'Ditherus darling!' interrupted Hilaria, bursting out of the crowd. 'What are you doing here?'

'I told you,' said Ditherus. 'I've been training as a gladiator. Didn't you see my fight?'

The Emperor was looking confused. 'Hang on a minute, you two know each other?'

'Of course we do,' said Hilaria. 'This is my son, Majesty.'

'This is young Dodderus?'

'Er, Ditherus, Majesty,' said Ditherus.

'Ditherus exactly,' said Porcus. 'I haven't seen you since that night at your house when I had you arrested.' His smile faded as some of the details came back to him. 'Come to think of it, shouldn't you be in prison?'

Ditherus took a deep breath. 'That was a mistake, Majesty,' he said. 'I swear it wasn't me that stole your sword.'

'Well, if it wasn't you, who in Hades was it?' demanded Porcus.

Tidio stepped forward. 'I think Marcus Furius can explain that, Excellency.'

Everyone turned to Furius, who stared at his feet sullenly and said nothing. Bladderax's arm tightened around his neck.

'You talk,' growled the barbarian. 'Tell mighty Sneezer the truth.'

'All right,' croaked Furius, struggling to breathe. '*It was me.*'

Porcus shook his head. 'You'll have to speak up a bit, Marcus, I can't hear a word you're saying!'

'I said IT WAS ME!' bellowed Furius, breaking free at last. 'I stole your precious sword and I made sure the boy got the blame.'

Porcus stared in surprise. 'But really, Marcus, wasn't that a bit mean?'

'MEAN? MEAN?' Furius's face was so red he looked like he might explode. 'I'll tell you what is mean, Highness. It's having to babysit a brainless turnip like you. Six years I've waited. Six years of bowing and scraping and tying your sandals for you. And when the time came who did you pick as general?'

'Um, remind me,' said Porcus.

'CAIUS WART, THAT'S WHO!' roared Furius.

'ALWAYS CAIUS AND NEVER ME!' Furius rushed at the Emperor as if he meant to throttle him. He might have succeeded if a giant fist hadn't got in his way, flattening him in the dust.

'Him bad man, Sneezer,' observed Bladderax. 'Make plenty big troubles. You want I feed him to lions?'

Porcus Maximus waved a jewelled hand. 'No, no, take him away. I'll deal with him in the morning.' Bladderax bowed and threw Furius over his shoulder like a sack of potatoes, carrying him off to the cells. The Emperor watched him go. 'Extraordinary!' he said.

'What is, Majesty?' asked Ditherus.

'That barbarian. Didn't you notice? He looks exactly like the one you killed.'

'Ah yes,' said Ditherus hastily. 'That's because it's, um . . . it's his brother, Majesty. They're twins.'

'Really? Twins? And both barbarians? Quite extraordinary!'

Porcus shook his head, before turning his attention back to Ditherus.

'As for you, young Dodderus, I think we owe you an apology.'

'Me, Majesty?' said Ditherus.

'Certainly, if it wasn't for you I might have arrested

your father instead of that raving lunatic, Furius. Only a complete nincompoop would do something like that, eh?'

'Well, yes . . . I mean no,' said Ditherus.

'So tell me how can I reward you? A medal? An elephant? They do make a mess but they're very useful for parades.'

'Actually, Your Highness,' said Ditherus, 'there is one thing I would like.'

'Name it, my dear boy,' said Porcus. 'Anything at all.'

Ditherus drew the Nemesis from his belt. 'This sword,' he said. 'It saved my life, so I was wondering if, well, I could keep it?'

Porcus laughed and put an arm round his

shoulder. 'My dear Ditherus, this shouldn't be gathering dust in a collection. A sword like this should belong to a hero!'

'Oh,' said Ditherus, 'I see.'

'Which is why,' beamed the Emperor, 'I am giving it to you!'

Ditherus took the legendary sword, glowing with pride. Wait till he showed this to his dad and brothers when they returned from the war. He raised it in the air and couldn't resist a bit of sword twirling to please the crowd.

'LOOK OUT!' cried Tidio, as the sword shot backwards, cartwheeling through the air. It sliced through a thick rope, which snapped in half with a loud twang.

'Whoops!' said Ditherus. 'I hope that wasn't anything . . .'

But before he could say 'important' the great canopy shading the arena came tumbling down on their heads like the sky falling in. There was a stunned silence as everyone bumbled around in the dark, bumping into each other.

'Ditherus darling,' sighed Hilaria. 'How many times have I warned you *not* to play with swords!'